The Three Little Magicians

The Three Little Magicians

Georgie Adams

Illustrated by Emily Bolam

Orion
Children's Books

First published in Great Britain in 2014
by Orion Children's Books
a division of the Orion Publishing Group Ltd
Orion House
5 Upper St Martin's Lane
London WC2H 9EA
An Hachette UK Company

1 3 5 7 9 10 8 6 4 2

ISBN 978 1 4440 1145 6

Printed in China

The Orion Publishing Group's policy is to use papers that are natural,
renewable and recyclable products made from wood grown in sustainable forests.
The logging and manufacturing processes are expected to conform
to the environmental regulations of the country of origin.

www.orionbooks.co.uk

For Tom Adams — a bit of a wizard!
With love, G. A.

Contents

Chapter 1
Meet the Magicians!

Presenting, for the first time, the fantastic little magicians – Miranda, Maisy and Max.

This is Miranda and her guinea pig, Trumps.

Here is Maisy and her cat, Marbles.

And this is Max. He has a rabbit called Gavin.

They all live together in Hey Presto! House.

One night, the three little magicians were woken by some loud noises.

WHEEEE! CRASH! BANG!

They jumped out of their beds and ran outside.

Their neighbour, Mr Marzipan, who was a very clever magician, had a strange green cloud over his roof.

Miranda, Maisy and Max found Mr Marzipan sitting on the floor. He had a bump on his head.

"I'll never win the competition now," said Mr Marzipan.

"What competition?" said Miranda.

"The Best Magic Show at the Crystal Castle," said Mr Marzipan.

The little magicians had heard about the show. They knew that only the most powerful magicians took part.

"I was working on my new trick," Mr Marzipan told them. "But suddenly, everything went wrong. I wouldn't be surprised if that horrible magician, Zigzag, had something to do with it. He's always trying to steal my tricks!"

The bump on Mr Marzipan's head was getting bigger.

"I don't feel very well," he said.

"Can we help?" said Miranda.

Mr Marzipan had an idea. It was such a crazy idea that it hurt his head to even think about it.

"Hoodlam boodlam!" he said. "It might just work."

Chapter 2
The Little Book of Magic

Mr Marzipan took something out of his pocket.

"This is my *Little Book of Magic*," he said. "All my best tricks are in here. I want you to learn my amazing new trick and enter The Best Magic Show!"

The three little magicians couldn't believe their ears.

"But you must promise to keep it a secret," said Mr Marzipan.

"Yes," they all said. "We promise."

"Good," said Mr Marzipan. "It's a tricky trick but I'm sure you can do it. I don't feel well enough to enter the competition. We can't let Zigzag win."

When Miranda opened the *Little Book of Magic* she was puzzled.

"There's nothing in it," she said.

"Ah ha!" said Mr Marzipan. "Just tap the book three times with your wand and say:

'Numbers, letters, words and phrases,

Write yourselves upon these pages!'

And the words will appear – like magic!"

He told them the competition was at the next Blue Moon.

Maisy looked at a calendar hanging on the wall. "The next Blue Moon is tomorrow night!" she said.

"Oh, help!" said Max. "Let's go."

Mr Marzipan pointed to a rolled-up carpet in a corner of the room.

"Take my flying carpet," he said. "It will get you to the show on time. The Crystal Castle is over the hills, on top of a mountain."

"Cool!" said Max. He couldn't wait to try it.

Chapter 3

Hocus Pocus

Next morning, Miranda, Maisy and Max were up early. They chatted excitedly as they ate bowls of Fruity Fizz Pops.

"All the stuff for the trick was destroyed in the explosion last night," said Miranda. "But we can buy everything at Hocus Pocus."

"My favourite shop!" said Maisy.

"What do we need?" said Max.

"It's in here," Miranda said, tapping Mr Marzipan's *Little Book of Magic* three times with her wand. They all said the magic words together:

'Numbers, letters, words and phrases,

Write yourselves upon these pages!'

The three little magicians checked the book carefully, then they ran to Hocus Pocus, the biggest magic store in town.

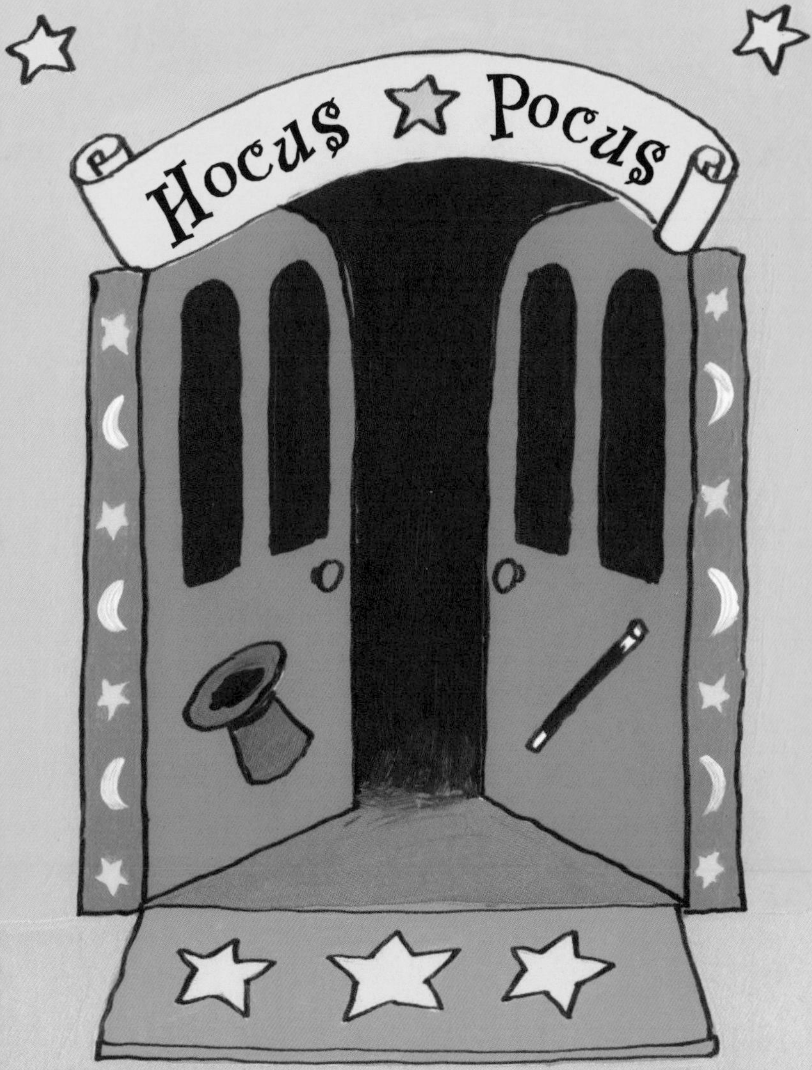
Hocus Pocus

The three little magicians were trying to find their way out when they bumped into a tall, mean-looking magician. It was none other than Mr Marzipan's arch-rival – Zigzag!

EXPERIENCED MAGICIANS ONLY

Uh-oh!

It's Zigzag.

"Can't you read?" snarled Zigzag. "This department is for experienced magicians only. What are **you** doing here?"

"Er, we got lost," said Miranda.

"We're just going," said Maisy.

He looks angry!

"Not so fast," Zigzag said. "What have you got there?"

"N-n-nothing much," said Max.

"B-b-bits and pieces," said Maisy.

"Well, I don't believe you," sneered Zigzag. "Tell me the truth, or else!"

But Miranda, Maisy and Max had promised Mr Marzipan to keep a secret. They didn't say a word.

Zigzag was hopping mad. He pointed his wand at them and said:

"Spat, spot, spit, spick —
Tell me the truth. Say it quick!"

Suddenly, the three little magicians felt very sleepy. In a dreamy daze, they told Zigzag about performing Mr Marzipan's trick at The Best Magic Show.

Luckily, Miranda woke up before Zigzag could snatch the *Little Book of Magic*. None of the three little magicians remembered what had happened. And Zigzag was nowhere to be seen.

SHOOTING STARS

"Come on," said Miranda. "Let's go
home. We've got lots to do before midnight!"

Chapter 4
Up, Up and Away!

The little magicians spent the rest of the day preparing for the show. Mr Marzipan's trick was *very* tricky!

They were working so hard that they didn't notice how late it was getting, until Maisy looked out of the window and cried: "It's night-time!"

"Hubble-bubble," said Miranda. "We have to be at the Crystal Castle by midnight!"

Max fetched Mr Marzipan's flying carpet and unrolled it.

The three little magicians put everything onto the carpet.

"Do you know how to fly this thing, Max?" said Miranda.

It'll never get off the ground!

It's got holes in it.

I'm not flying on that old thing!

"I couldn't find any instructions," said Max. "But there's a label with a funny rhyme."

He read it aloud:

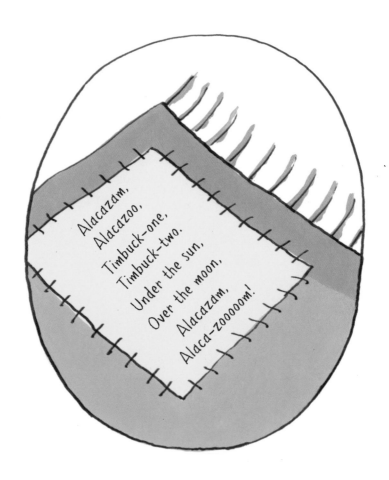

Alacazam,
Alacazoo,
Timbuck-one,
Timbuck-two.
Under the sun,
Over the moon,
Alacazam,
Alaca-zooooom!

The flying carpet gave a shake. Then, very slowly, it rose into the air.

"We're off!" cried Max.

"It works!" said Maisy.

"Hold onto your hats!" said Miranda.

The flying carpet flew higher and higher, over the rooftops and into the night sky. The three little magicians sang happily as they flew:

*"Up, up and away we go —
all the way to the magic show!"*

Chapter 5
Lost in Space!

The flying carpet was zooming along, when suddenly the three little magicians were caught up in a whirlwind.

whooOOOooo!
whooOOOooo!

The whirlwind spun them round and round.

"Hubble-bubble!" said Miranda. "What's happening?"

"I don't know," said Max.

"I'm falling!" cried Maisy.

The magicians heard someone laugh in a nasty way. When they looked down, they saw Zigzag!

"Ha ha! My whirlwind spell is working," said Zigzag. "I must have that *Little Book of Magic!*"

The flying carpet flipped. Miranda was tossed like a pancake in a pan, and the *Little Book of Magic* slipped from her pocket.

"Oh no!" she cried.

"It's gone!" said Maisy.

"Got it!" cried Zigzag. "Ha ha! I'll definitely win the competition now."

He pointed his wand at the flying carpet and sent Miranda, Maisy and Max shooting towards the stars.

Chapter 6
The Magic Moonbeam

"We're heading for the Blue Moon!" cried Max, trying to steer the carpet.

"We'll never make it to the competition now," said Maisy.

"It's not fair!" said Miranda.

The three little magicians could see the Crystal Castle far below them, but they couldn't stop the flying carpet.

Then Max gave a shout: "Look!"

A bright blue moonbeam had appeared.
It stretched like a silvery pathway, right down
to the Crystal Castle.

The carpet landed on the moonbeam,
then it began to slide . . .

Inside the Crystal Castle, the most powerful magicians in the world were getting ready for the show.

Zigzag was there too. He couldn't wait to perform Mr Marzipan's trick.

He opened the *Little Book of Magic*.

To his surprise, there wasn't a squiggle, a dot or a mark inside. Not a word.

Zigzag stamped his foot and threw the *Little Book of Magic* on the floor.

Many marvellous magicians took part in the competition.

But things did not go well for Zigzag. He hadn't brought quite enough of Whizzo's Invisible Paint to make himself disappear.

And when he tried to saw his assistant in half, things went from bad to worse.

Rick-rack-rick-rack! went the saw.

"Ouch! Ooo! Ow!" yelled the poor woman who was inside the box.

The audience booed.

"Rubbish!" they cried. "Get off!"

Zigzag ran from the castle as fast as he could. He could never show his face there again.

Just when everyone thought the show was over — *Wheeeee! Thump-thump-thump!*

Miranda, Maisy and Max came sliding down a moonbeam and landed on the stage.

Chapter 7

Three Little Super Stars!

"Ladies and gentlemen! Boys and girls!"
said Miranda. "We are The Three Little
Magicians!"

The little magicians began by doing a few simple tricks of their own.

Miranda turned silk handkerchiefs into butterflies that flew around the stage.

Maisy took some bright balloons and turned them into a bunch of flowers.

And when Max tapped his wand and cried: "Ta daaa!" Gavin sprang from a top hat.

The audience clapped after each perfect performance.

"Now for Mr Marzipan's special trick!" Miranda whispered to Maisy and Max.

First, Miranda and Maisy started juggling with balls.

Then Max threw handfuls of glittery
stardust into the air, waved his wand and said:
"Funtastic! Fantazzimo!
Balls fizz and whizzio!"

There was a loud **bang** and everyone jumped.

The sparkling, spinning balls had turned into shooting stars.

The audience cheered and clapped. It was the most spectacular trick they had ever seen.

At the end, the Grand Wizard presented the prizes.

"And the winners of The Best Magic Show competition are . . . The Three Little Magicians!" he said.

As they were leaving, Miranda saw something lying on the floor, at the side of the stage. It was Mr Marzipan's *Little Book of Magic*!

The next day, Miranda, Maisy and Max gave their prize to Mr Marzipan. After all, it was his trick that had helped them win the competition.

"Well done, little magicians!" Mr Marzipan said.

"We nearly didn't get to the show," said Maisy.

"Zigzag cast a horrid spell," said Miranda.

"Luckily, a moonbeam . . ." began Max.

Mr Marzipan smiled. "I've been keeping an eye on you through my crystal ball," he said. "I do have a few tricks up my sleeve, you know!"

So now we must leave them all and say:

"Goodbye,
Miranda."

"Goodbye,
Maisy."

"Goodbye,
Max."

Goodbye, little magicians.
Goodbye!

What are you going to read next?

Have more adventures with Horrid Henry,

or save the day with Anthony Ant!

Become a superhero with Monstar,

float off to sea with Algy,

or have your very own Pirates' Picnic.

Grow carrots with

Lottie and Dottie,

make magic with The Witch Dog,

and cast a spell with

The Three Little Magicians.

Enjoy all the Early Readers.